# GIRLS ROCK!

# Dance Fever

## Holly Smith Dinbergs

illustrated by
## Chantal Stewart

## RISING★STARS

First published in Great Britain by
RISING STARS UK LTD 2008
22 Grafton Street, London W1S 4EX

For information visit our website at:
www.risingstars-uk.com

British Library Cataloguing in Publication Data
A CIP record for this book is available from the British Library.

ISBN: 978 1 84680 267 6

First published in 2008 by
MACMILLAN EDUCATION AUSTRALIA PTY LTD
15–19 Claremont Street, South Yarra 3141

Visit our website at www.macmillan.com.au

Associated companies and representatives throughout the world.

Series created by Felice Arena and Phil Kettle
Project management by Limelight Publishing Services Pty Ltd
Cover and text design by Lore Foye
Illustrations by Chantal Stewart

Printed in China

# GIRLS ROCK!
# Contents

*Jess*     *Sophie*

# CHAPTER 1

# **Radio Problem**

Best friends Sophie and Jess are sitting
on the floor in Sophie's bedroom on a
rainy Saturday morning. Jess holds a
gigantic lollipop. Jess's cocker spaniel
Sammy is napping next to the girls.

**Jess**  "Why are you frowning?"

**Sophie**  "Everybody's going to think I'm an idiot."

**Jess**  "What are you talking about?"

Jess takes a big lick of her lollipop.

**Sophie**  "I'm going to look ridiculous!"

**Jess**  "Like when I wore my shirt inside out on the day they took the class photo?"

**Sophie**  "No. I'm talking total disaster."

**Jess**  "Like when I threw up at school? Now, that was total disaster!"

**Sophie** "Yeah, that was bad—but
that was kid stuff. My cousin's
having a party next week."
**Jess** (puzzled) "But you like parties."

Jess stands up and turns on
Sophie's radio. The loud music wakes
up Sammy.

**Sophie** "I used to like parties. Now I hate them."

**Jess** "What's the problem? Wait, I know. You need new shoes."

**Sophie** "No. Shoes are not my problem. That's the problem."

She points at the radio.

**Jess** "Your radio is the problem?"

**Sophie** "Not the radio. The music."

**Jess** "The music?"

**Sophie** "It's a dance party. I don't know how to dance. Everyone will laugh at me."

**Jess** "No they won't. Dancing's fun."

**Sophie** "Not for me it isn't!"

**Jess** "Well, I can change that."

**Sophie** "How?"

# CHAPTER 2

# Coach Jess

Sophie waits eagerly for Jess to explain her plan.

**Jess** "I'm going to be your dance coach. I'm going to teach you everything I know."

**Sophie** (excited)  "Really? You really think you can do that?"

**Jess**  "Sure. But we can't do it here."

She looks around Sophie's room and sees her bed, desk, bike and beanbag chair.

**Jess** "We need more room. Let's go to
the lounge."

**Sophie** "Okay."

**Jess** "Come on, Sammy."

The girls and Sammy head for the
door, until Sophie stops short. Jess
almost crashes into her and falls
over. Sammy crashes into Jess.

**Jess** "Give me some warning, why don't you?"

**Sophie** "If we're in the lounge, my brother might see us."

**Jess** "Who cares?"

**Sophie** "Me. That's who! He'll make fun of me."

**Jess** "He's not even home."
**Sophie** (laughing) "Oh, right. I forgot. Let's go."

As the girls walk downstairs, the front door opens and in walks Sophie's brother. He walks past the girls, acting as if he doesn't see them.

# CHAPTER 3

# Flash One

Jess turns to Sophie.

**Jess** "He didn't even say hello. See? He doesn't care what we're doing."

**Sophie** "You don't know him. He sees everything. If he can find a new way to torture me, he will."

The girls walk into the lounge.
Jess turns on the radio and tunes in
to her favourite station.

**Jess** "I loooooove this song. Perfect.
Now watch me."

Jess waves her arms, shakes her
hips, and moves her head from side
to side.

**Sophie** "How do you know what to do?"

**Jess** "I don't. I just do whatever I feel like. Try it."

**Sophie** "It's too embarrassing."

**Jess** "Soph, give it a try! Nobody's watching. Start moving."

**Sophie** "But I don't know what to do!"

**Jess** "Okay, okay. Then … pretend you're swatting away a bee."

Sophie moves her arms, pretending to swat a bee.

**Jess** "Cool! Now pretend you're head-butting a football."

Sophie moves her head as if she's butting a football.

**Jess** "Get your feet moving! Pretend you're squashing some bugs."

Following Jess's suggestions, Sophie is moving her arms, head and feet to the music. Sammy runs around the room barking.

**Jess** "You're getting the hang of it!"
**Sophie** "How do I look?"
**Jess** "Like J. Lo."

Just then, the girls are blinded by a bright flash of light. They freeze.

**Jess** "What was that?"
**Sophie** "That was my loser brother, and he just took a picture of us with his new camera. We have to get that camera!"

# CHAPTER 4

# Flash Two

Sophie strides up and down the lounge, muttering.

**Jess** "Soph, I think you're going a little mental here. Who cares about your stupid brother's picture?"

**Sophie** "I do! He'll show that picture to everybody. Come on."

Sophie runs upstairs, followed by Jess and Sammy. Sophie stops in front of her brother's bedroom door and pounds on it with her fist. Sammy barks.

**Sophie** (shouting)  "Open up, you creep. Give me that camera!"

Sophie's brother responds by turning up his music really loud.

**Jess** (shouting)  "Sophie, this isn't working."

**Sophie**  "We're going to get his attention. Follow me."

Sophie leads Jess downstairs and out of the front door. Sammy is close at their heels.

**Jess** "Where are we going?"
**Sophie** "The garden."

Sophie stops in the middle of the garden and stoops to pick up a few pebbles. She throws them at her brother's window.

**Sophie** "I know you're in there! I want that camera!"

**Jess** "Soph, you're so mad, your eyes look like they're going to pop out of your head. Not a pretty picture."

Suddenly, the girls are blinded by another bright flash—this time coming from her brother's window.

**Sophie** "He did it again. He took our picture!"

**Jess** "That light was right in my eyes. I can't see anything. I can't see! Help me, I can't see!"

Jess closes her eyes and walks around the garden, pretending she can't see. She trips over Sammy and falls to the ground. Sammy runs over and licks her face. The girls burst out laughing.

**Jess** "This is crazy. Let's go back inside. I have a new plan."

# CHAPTER 5

# Flash You

The girls walk back into the lounge.

**Sophie** "So what's your plan?"
**Jess** "You have a camera, right?"
**Sophie** "Yeah."

**Jess** "Isn't your brother's room right next to yours?"

**Sophie** "Yeah … and?"

**Jess** "And if you stand out on your balcony, can't you see right into his room? I wonder what's he up to in there."

**Sophie** "Brilliant! I like how you think. Come on."

The girls run upstairs to Sophie's
room. Sophie digs her camera out
from the bottom of her desk drawer.
Jess stands out on the balcony
and peers into Sophie's brother's
bedroom.

**Jess** (whispering)  "I don't believe it!"
**Sophie**  "What? What's he doing?"

Sophie leans over Jess's shoulder
and sees her brother dancing in front
of a mirror.

**Sophie** "I've never seen him do that
before!"

**Jess** "Yeah, it looks like your brother
has caught himself a good case of
dance fever. Look at him go. Well,
at least he's having fun!"

**Sophie** "What? Are you serious?!"

**Jess** "Yeah, I am. That's what I've
been trying to tell you, Soph.
Dancing is meant to be fun. Who
cares what you look like?"

**Sophie** "My brother will. Just
watch this."

Sophie aims her camera. *FLASH!* Sophie's brother looks shocked as he is caught in the bright light. The girls pop back into the room and run for it. Sophie's brother chases after them.

**Sophie** "Thanks, Jess."

**Jess** "For what?"

**Sophie** "You're right, dancing is fun. And this was totally worth it!"

# GIRLS ROCK!
# Dance Lingo

*Jess*                                    *Sophie*

**choreographer** Fancy word for anyone who makes up dance routines. (Ask your mum or dad how to pronounce it.)

**dressing room** A room backstage where you get dressed and do your make-up and hair before, during or after a dance performance.

**dress rehearsal** The last rehearsal of a dance, in costume with all the lights and sets, before the real performance.

**professional** Anybody who gets paid for dancing—like the people who dance with J. Lo in her video clips. A professional is often called a "pro".

**step** What you do each time you move your feet while you dance.

# GIRLS ROCK!
# Dance Must-dos

☆ Smile and look confident when you dance, and everyone will think you know exactly what you are doing, even if you don't!

☆ Move around or stretch before you start dancing so that your muscles will be nice and warm—and you will move better.

☆ Eat some fruit or a muesli bar if you need some energy (not sweets), and drink water before a dance class or performance.

☆ Dance in front of the mirror to check out your own moves. You'll see what a superstar you are!

☆ If you hurt anywhere (like your foot or ankle) while you are dancing, stop dancing and tell your mum or dad. Pain is how your body tells you, "Stop what you are doing!"

☆ Make sure you have a really cool outfit to dance in. You will look like a professional dancer (and feel like one, too).

☆ Tell your mum and dad that you need to see a lot of dance performances, so that you can decide on your favourite dance style. It's important for your dancing career!

☆ To find the rhythm, tap your toes until you find the beat. Once you find that, start moving the rest of your body.

# Dance Instant Info

♪ Dancers need to be really flexible and strong so that they can keep dancing for hours at a time.

♪ Professional dancers train and practise an average of six hours a day (and do other things like lift weights, martial arts and yoga to improve physical fitness and technique).

♪ Because dancing is so hard on the body, lots of dancers stop dancing professionally before they reach age 40.

♪ A tap-dancing world record was set in Germany in 1998, when 6952 tap dancers tapped together for 2 minutes and 15 seconds to honour the memory of Bill "Bojangles" Robinson, a famous tap dancer.

♪ People traditionally say, "break a leg" to wish a dancer good luck before a performance. Why? Because the dance world is superstitious and if you say, "break a leg" to a dancer, it means that you hope the opposite will happen.

♪ If you are dancing in a show, you can relax in a quiet room backstage called the Green Room in between performances. The Green Room may not actually be green, but it's the room where dancers and other performers hang out and greet their fans.

♪ The phrase, "Dancers to your places" is what dancers listen for to announce the start of the performance.

# GIRLS ROCK!
# Think Tank

1 How long do professional dancers train each day?

2 What's the best kind of dancing?

3 What do you say to a professional dancer to wish her good luck before a performance?

4 What kind of exercises do you do before your dance class or performance?

5 Who makes up dance routines?

6 What is the best outfit to wear when you dance?

7 Where can you go to relax in between dance performances?

8 What phrase signals the start of a dance performance?

# Answers

## How did you score?

- If you got all 8 answers correct, you are ready to audition for a dancing role in your favourite singer's next video clip.

- If you got 6 answers correct, you can show off your best moves to your friends the next time you are invited to a dance party.

- If you got fewer than 4 answers correct, you'd better close the curtains the next time you dance in the lounge.

*Hey Girls!*

*I hope you had fun reading this story. You know what I love most about reading? I can open a book and read a fantastic story about funny people or cool animals without even moving. And I can read wherever I want—in my room, in the library, in the park— anywhere. (When I was little, I tried to read in the car, but it made me feel sick. If that happens to you, ask your mum or dad about using some headphones to listen to books recorded on CDs.)*

*You can have even more fun if you read "Dance Fever" out loud with somebody else— like your best friend or mum or dad. Here's another idea—you and your class can use this story to put on a play.*

To bring the story to life, get some cool props. What would work for this story? A flashlight (a pretend camera)? A stuffed dog? A radio?

Who will be Jess? Who will be Sophie? Who will be the narrator? (That's the person who reads the parts between when Jess or Sophie says something.). Maybe a talent scout will visit your class and you'll be invited to Hollywood for a movie audition. No matter what happens, you'll have fun!

You know what my dad used to tell me? Readers are leaders. So keep reading!

And, always remember—Boys may think they rule, but *Girls Rock!*

*Holly Smith Dilberg*

# When We Were Kids

Holly     Jacqueline

Holly talked to Jacqueline, another *Girls Rock!* author.

**Jacqueline** "Did you always like to dance?"

**Holly** "Yeah! In my room to the radio when nobody was home. I used to watch people on the telly and try to imitate them."

**Jacqueline** "Who did you dance with?"

**Holly** "Sometimes my best friend. Sometimes my dog."

**Jacqueline** "Was your dog a good dancer?"

**Holly** "He barked a lot."

**Jacqueline** "Maybe that was his way of saying, 'You're a good dancer'."

**Holly** "I think it was more his way of saying, 'Can I have a snack?'."

# What a Laugh!

**Q** What makes cows dance?

**A** Any really great moo-sic!

# GIRLS ROCK!

Read about the fun that girls have in these *GIRLS ROCK!* titles:

**Birthday Party Blues**
**Pony Club**

**Doubles Trouble**
**Football Crazy**

**Dance Fever**
**Minigolf Face-off**

**Trapeze Dreams**
**Two at the Zoo**

... and 20 more great titles to choose from!

*GIRLS ROCK!* books are available from most booksellers. For mail order information please call Rising Stars on 0871 47 23 010 or visit www.risingstars-uk.com

44